This book belongs to

_____

MOTHER GOOSE'S NURSERY RHYMES

THE CAT AND THE FIDDLE

AND OTHER FAVORITES

ILLUSTRATED BY
ALLEN ATKINSON

AN ARIEL BOOK

BANTAM BOOKS

TORONTO · NEW YORK · LONDON · SYDNEY · AUCKLAND

THE CAT AND THE FIDDLE AND OTHER FAVORITES
A Bantam Book
April 1985

Art Direction: Armand Eisen and Tom Durwood

ISBN 0-553-15321-8

Published simultaneously in the United States and Canada

Bantam Books are published by Bantam Books, Inc. Its trademark,
consisting of the words "Bantam Books" and the portrayal of a rooster, is
Registered in U.S. Patent and Trademark Office and in other countries.
Marca Registrada. Bantam Books, Inc., 666 Fifth Avenue, New York,
New York 10103.

Printing and binding by
Printer, industria gráfica S.A.   Provenza, 388   Barcelona
Depósito legal B. 334-1985
PRINTED IN SPAIN
0 9 8 7 6 5 4 3 2 1

"No, no, my melodies will never die,
While nurses sing or babies cry."
　　　　　—Mother Goose

HEY DIDDLE, diddle,
The cat and the fiddle,
The cow jumped over the moon;
The little dog laughed
To see such sport
And the dish ran away with the spoon.

SING A SONG of sixpence,
A pocket full of rye,
Four and twenty blackbirds
Baked in a pie.

MOTHER GOOSE'S NURSERY RHYMES

MOTHER GOOSE'S NURSERY RHYMES

When the pie was opened,
The birds began to sing;
Was not that a dainty dish,
To set before the king?

The king was in his counting-house,
Counting out his money;
The queen was in the parlor,
Eating bread and honey;

The maid was in the garden,
Hanging out the clothes,
When along came a blackbird,
And snapped off her nose.

Along came a Jenny Wren
And popped it on again.

MOTHER GOOSE'S NURSERY RHYMES

LITTLE JACK HORNER
Sat in a corner,
Eating a Christmas pie;
He put in his thumb,
And pulled out a plum,
And said, What a good boy am I.

THERE WAS A crooked man,
And he walked a crooked mile,
He found a crooked sixpence
Against a crooked stile;
He bought a crooked cat,
Which caught a crooked mouse,
And they all lived together
In a little crooked house.

I SAW A SHIP a-sailing,
A-sailing on the sea,
And oh but it was laden,
With pretty things for thee.

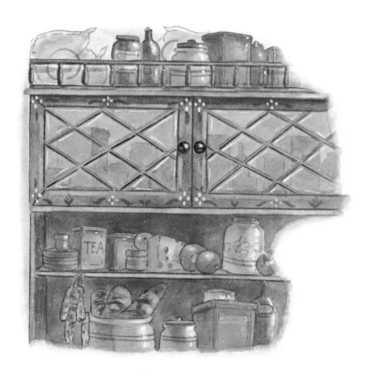

There were comfits in the cabin,
And apples in the hold;
The sails were made of silk,
And the masts were all of gold.

The four-and-twenty sailors,
That stood between the decks,
Were four-and-twenty white mice
With chains about their necks.

The captain was a duck
With a packet on his back,
And when the ship began to move
The captain said Quack! Quack!

LITTLE MISS MUFFET
Sat on a tuffet,
Eating her curds and whey;
Along came a spider
Who sat down beside her
And frightened Miss Muffet away.

MOTHER GOOSE'S NURSERY RHYMES

OLD WOMAN, old woman,
>shall we go a-shearing?
Speak a little louder, sir,
>I'm very hard of hearing.

Old woman, old woman,
>shall we go a-gleaning?
Speak a little louder, sir,
>I cannot tell your meaning.

Old woman, old woman,
>shall I kiss you dearly?
Thank you, kind sir,
>I hear you very clearly.

Old woman, old woman,
>shall we go a-walking?
Speak a little louder, sir,
>or what's the use of talking?

ONE MISTY, moisty morning,
When cloudy was the weather,
I chanced to meet an old man
Clothed all in leather,
Clothed all in leather,
With strap under his chin.
How do you do, and how do you do,
And how do you do again?

To MARKET, to market, to buy a fat pig,
Home again, home again, jiggety-jig;
To market, to market, to buy a fat hog,
Home again, home again, jiggety-jog.

MOSES SUPPOSES his toeses are roses,
But Moses supposes erroneously;
For nobody's toeses are posies of roses
As Moses supposes his toeses to be.

PETER PIPER picked a peck of pickled pepper;
A peck of pickled pepper Peter Piper picked.
If Peter Piper picked a peck of pickled pepper,
Where's the
       peck
           of pickled
               pepper
                   Peter Piper
                       picked?

MOTHER GOOSE'S NURSERY RHYMES

DIDDLE, DIDDLE, dumpling, my son John
Went to bed with his trousers on;
One shoe off, and one shoe on,
Diddle, diddle, dumpling, my son John.

THERE WAS A FROG liv'd in a well,
Kitty alone, Kitty alone,
There was a frog liv'd in a well,
Kitty alone and I.
There was a frog liv'd in a well,
And a farce mouse in a mill,
Cock me cary, Kitty alone,
Kitty alone and I.

This frog he would a wooing ride,
Kitty alone, Kitty alone,
This frog he would a wooing ride,
Kitty alone and I.
This frog he would a wooing ride,
And on a snail he got astride,
Cock me cary, Kitty alone,
Kitty alone and I.

He rode till he came to my Lady Mouse hall,
Kitty alone, Kitty alone,
He rode till he came to my Lady Mouse hall,
Kitty alone and I.
He rode till he came to my Lady Mouse hall,
And there he did both knock and call,
Cock me cary, Kitty alone,
Kitty alone and I.

SOLOMON GRUNDY,
Born on a Monday,
Christened on Tuesday,
Married on Wednesday,
Took ill on Thursday,
Worse on Friday,
Died on Saturday,
Buried on Sunday.
This is the end
Of Solomon Grundy.

JENNY WREN last week was wed,
And built her nest in grandpa's shed;
Look in next week and you shall see
Two little eggs, and maybe three.

NOSE, NOSE, jolly red nose,
And what gave thee that jolly red nose?
Nutmeg and ginger, cinnamon and cloves,
That's what gave me this jolly red nose.

MOTHER GOOSE'S NURSERY RHYMES

LONDON BRIDGE is falling down,
Falling down, falling down.
London bridge is falling down,
My fair lady.

SLEEP, BABY, SLEEP,
Thy father guards the sheep;
Thy mother shakes the dreamland tree,
And from it fall sweet dreams for thee.
Sleep, baby, sleep.

MOTHER GOOSE'S NURSERY RHYMES

Sleep, baby, sleep,
Our cottage vale is deep;
The little lamb is on the green,
With woolly fleece so soft and clean.
Sleep, baby, sleep.

MOTHER GOOSE'S NURSERY RHYMES

Sleep, baby, sleep,
Down where the woodbines creep;
Be always like the lamb so mild,
A kind and sweet and gentle child,
Sleep, baby, sleep.